A Princess of Great Daring!

Written by Tobi Hill-Meyer

Illustrated by Elenore Toczynski

Jamie hadn't seen her very best friends Liam, Jackson, and Madison all summer. She was very excited that she'd see them in just a few more minutes.

"Are you sure you're ready to tell your friends that you're a girl now?" asked her Mama E.

"Are you sure you don't want us to help you tell them?" asked her Mama M.

"It's okay," Jamie said, "I'll be fine."

When they got to Jackson's house, Liam, Jackson, and Madison were already playing.
"If you need to come home early you know you can call us," her moms said.
"I know" Jamie said. She hopped out of the car and ran to join her friends.

"Jamie! You're just in time!" Madison yelled. "We're playing rescue the princess!"

"Yeah," Liam said. "We each get to be princes or knights and we're going to fight a dragon."

"I'm going to be a smart and strategic prince who always knows just what to say," said Jackson.

"I'm going to be a charming and beautiful prince who everyone wants to be friends with," said Liam.

"I'm going to be a brave and strong knight who can beat anyone in a fight," said Madison.

They all turned to Jamie. "What kind of prince are you going to be?"

"Uh, I'm going to be a princess," said Jamie.

"That's perfect!" said Madison. "We can all come and rescue you!"

"No, that's not the kind of princess I'm going to be," said Jamie. "I'm going to be a princess of great daring! I can climb and run and keep up with any of you."

"I'll wear the most beautiful dresses for parties with Liam, I'll challenge Jackson's wits in chess, and Madison and I will train together to be strong. And the four of us will be the best friends across the land."

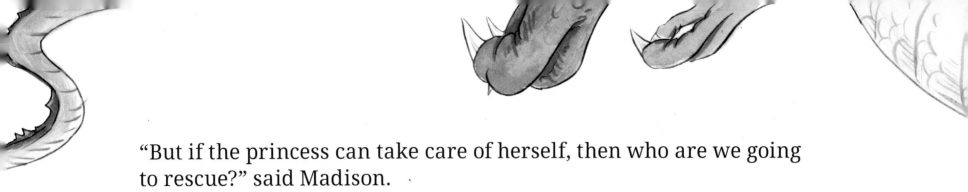

"But if the princess can take care of herself, then who are we going to rescue?" said Madison.

"What if you all rescued me?" said Liam.

"Perfect," said Jackson. "We'll all be hanging out at the castle, having tea. Out of nowhere, a dragon swoops down and grabs Liam and flies away!"

"Quick, we must see where it is going!" said Jackson.

"I know!" said Jamie, "I'll climb the castle wall."

"You're still not high enough."

"I'll jump to a nearby tree and climb to the top!"

"Where did the dragon go?" said Jackson.

"Into a cave by the mountains," said Jamie.

"Well let's go chase it, and rescue Liam!" said Madison.

"It takes almost all day to make it to the cave, but now there is a giant boulder blocking it," said Jackson.

"No problem!" said Madison, "I can push it out of the way!"

"There's a giant door behind the boulder," said Jackson.

Madison yelled: "I charge forward and knock the door down!"

"How should we deal with the dragon?" asked Jackson.

"We'll fight it!" said Madison. "The three of us can take anything!"

"But dragons are really big," said Jamie. "Maybe we can sneak past it."

"I know what to do," said Jackson. "I'm going to talk to it."

"Dragon!" called out Jackson. "Tell us why you've kidnapped our friend."

"Wait, it's okay!" yelled Liam. "The dragon's name is Jessica and she was just feeling lonely and wanted to ask me how I have so many friends – but now she refuses to let me go."

"Jackson, you should tell the dragon we can be her friends," said Jamie.

"I will," said Jackson. "But first I need to have a long conversation with the dragon. We will talk about our families and find things we have in common, and then I'll find out what is making her so sad. Finally, I'll tell her we can all be her friends but only if she can play nice and stop kidnapping people."

"Hooray," said Liam. "But also I hurt my foot when she flew me away, so I need someone to carry me all the way back."

"That was an awesome game, I'm really glad to see you all again," said Jamie.

"I'm glad you're back, too," said Madison. "You make a really awesome princess."

"Thanks," said Jamie. "That's probably because I'm really a girl - even though people always thought I was a boy since I was born. I wanted to tell you today, because next week I have to tell all the people at school."

"Is there something we should do that could help?" asked Jackson.

"Well, you can be sure to say 'she' and 'her' when you talk about me," Jamie said. "And if someone says 'Why is that boy wearing a dress?' you can say: 'That's our friend Jamie and she's a girl!'

I think it will be okay," Jamie said. "I'm just a little nervous."

"Well, lucky for you, you have a strong knight on your side," said Madison.

"And a clever diplomat," said Jackson.

"And a cheerful charmer!" said Liam.

And then they went back to playing. The four of them really were the best friends in the land, and they always knew just how to help each other.